Miracles

from the

Heart

J.Paulette Forshey

DISCLAIMER

All the characters in this book have no existence outside the imagination of the author and have no relation whatsoever to anyone bearing the same name or names. They are not even distantly inspired by any individual known or unknown to the author, and all incidents are pure invention.

Website: www.JPauletteForshey.com

Cover design: Danielle Zwissler

Editor: PS Ritchey DBA: Old Mill Publishing
    oldmillpublishing@gmail.com

Also By J. Paulette Forshey

A Tango Trinity

Cat and the Wizard

Passionate Cooks

The Estate

33 Days Til Christmas

ACKNOWLEDGEMENTS

My heartfelt thanks to Pam Ritchey's Old Mill
Publishing and the many hats she wears as editor,
formatter, and genius that understands geek speak.
And to Danielle Zwissler for the fantastic cover she
blessed on this book

CONTENTS

The Christmas Gift

by J.Paulette Forshey

Dedicated
To Belle
Loved and missed.
04/12/2002 – 03/03/2012

Present Day – Collette's Story

Collette ignored the cell phone ringing in her coat pocket and the cold air drying the tears on her cheeks leaving frigid tracks behind. She didn't bother to brush them away. Alone and empty, she'd once thought money and security would be enough to fill her life. Today had taught her otherwise. She choked back the sob in her throat in a painful gulp.

"Belle, I'm so sorry," she whispered to the sky and hugged her arms around her waist. She trudged down the path connecting her neighbor's, Mr. Stockwell, farm and her husband's estate, as snow softly fell on her face and eyelashes.

"How could he? Mr. Stockwell knew I was bringing more money today. How could he?" One foot in front of the other, she stumbled back down the trail, biting back another sob. The worst week of her life had started with Millicent Birdwell and her nasty group of so-called friends calling her horrible names followed by the loss of the little dog. It had all ended in a spectacular crash and burn, killing the last bit of hope in her heart for any type of family.

Five Years Ago – Colette

Abandoned by friends, family and left without a home she tried the shelter in her home town, arriving with two suitcases and twenty dollars in her pocket. The shelter turned out to be more dangerous than sleeping on the street. Her first night in the place, someone stole one of her bags. When she reported the theft, the person in charge of the housing offered protection...for a price. Colette had been inexperienced, but she knew what the man meant. Quietly, when no one was looking, she took her remaining possessions and disappeared into the night. Since finding herself on the streets and living out of a dilapidated storage unit, Colette had taken to standing in the shadows and eavesdropping on some of the streetwalkers. They'd been a wealth of information to her staying alive.

Six months later, the nights were becoming longer and much colder. Colette knew she would not last sleeping in the shed, but her first priority was food. Hopefully, she'd found a way to solve the food problem, even if it was for one night.

The hookers had spoken about a party being held tonight in the big estate on the edge of town. One of the girls bragged of how she'd snuck in at the last party, mingled with the guests, and eaten enough hors d'oeuvres to keep hunger at bay for a week. All before being discovered and tossed out. The prostitute also repeated the threat the security guard had promised her if she ever tried the stunt again. Fluffing her blond wig with the inch-long red fingernails, the streetwalker said she'd looked into the security guard's face and seeing his deadly stare, taken the threat seriously.

Colette couldn't, wouldn't sell herself like the others had, but she was so hungry. After listening to the women, she'd slipped back to the abandoned shed housing her and what little she owned. Gathering the only dress she owned and the matching shoes, she headed to the gas station nearby and their bathroom. She quickly washed her hair, bathed in the sink and then slipped on the clothes. She used the automatic hand dryer to dry her hair. With care, she applied the siren red lip stick that matched the dress. The dress, which clung to her slim form, shimmered in the dull yellow florescent light. Colette gently slid her fingertips over the silky material. It had cost a small fortune, this tiny bit of cloth, but her mother had purchased it for her saying she'd look smashing in it on her date with Dillon. Colette had never gotten to wear the dress or go out with Dillon. He'd run like a rabbit after her *misfortune* had been made public, and he'd never come by again. The coward hadn't even bothered to return her phone calls or emails, pretty much like her so-called relatives.

Checking her reflection in the broken mirror one more time, she then hurried off to the estate, hiding in the shadows outside the gates to wait for her chance. When the gates opened to permit a car's entrance, she slipped neatly through the opening and onto the grounds. There were many people coming and going. No one noticed an extra guest, and when she stepped through the door to the mansion with a couple, no one thought to ask her for an invitation.

She made sure not to stay in one spot for too long; nor did she linger overly at the buffet table. The food had been delicious and there was plenty of it, so much so that she thought she was safe going back one more time.

"Good evening." His voice, smooth, rich, and deep, came from behind her.

The hair on the back of her neck stood up and she turned slowly. "Hello." Perhaps he was just interested in her because of the dress color, strapless and oh, way too short hugging her thin shape, accenting every curve and swell. "I think you should come with me."

"I don't think my fiancé would like it if..." This had to be the security guard the hooker had spoken of, so Colette had to think fast.

"Nice try, but you're not here with anyone; in fact you're not even on the guest list. I know because I personally handpicked the guests." He took the plate from her hand and placed it on the table, then grasped her just above the elbow and pulled her along with him as he left the room. He didn't say another word until they reached what Colette thought was a study or library, where he none too gently shoved her into a high wingback chair.

"How did you get in here?" he growled. He was a tall man towering over her five-foot-eight stature by a good foot. Colette was grateful when he strode over to a desk putting some distance between them and then leaned back against it. He next proceeded to unbutton the jacket of his expensive tailored suit, folded his arms over his chest, and crossed his legs at the ankles. Relaxed, he exuded a powerful, feral elegance. "You might as well start talking, or would you rather wait for the police."

"Police? Can't you just let me leave? I'll never do anything like this again, I promise."

"What is your name?" he bit out.

"Colette, Colette Carpenter. Please, sir, I'll do anything you want. Please don't call the police."

She flinched from the stare he'd pinned her with; she knew he'd heard about her.

He ran the tip of his tongue over his lower lip and she watched mesmerized as he drawled, "Anything? Are you sure you want to offer me anything? Do you even know who you are offering *anything* to?"

Colette looked into his eyes and shivered from the coldness lying there, but right now that was better than the law. "No." She, in fact, had believed at the time he was the dreaded security guard. "Please don't call the police. I have nowhere else to go."

A tiny bit of warmth leaked into the iciness of his gaze, melting the hardness there, and it gave her hope.

"Why are you here?" He shifted and spread his legs wide.

"Food, free food."

"Nothing in life is free." The man let his arms drop to his sides, hands resting on the table behind him.

"I'm finding that out."

"Where are you living?"

She hung her head whispering, "In an old storage shed."

"Eating?" He straightened.

'Garbage bins outside of restaurants."

"I can fix all your problems."

"Really?"she said incredulously.

"All you have to do is say yes.

"To what?"

"Marry me."

"Marry you?"

"That's all you have to do."

"But why me?"

"Let's say I think you have potential. Say yes, and we leave as soon as the last guest departs. Oh, by the way, I'm Alexander Neuville, the host of this party, and owner of this home."

"Excuse me? Alexander who? Did you say marriage?"

"Like I said, say yes and we leave as soon as the last guest departs."

"Leave? For where?"

"Vegas, where we will be married, and before dawn you will be mine. So what is your decision?"

Colette sat there staring at him in disbelief.

"Times running out, Colette. Make your decision now." He reached for the phone on the desk.

The thought of returning to the shed, the cold, and fighting off the vermin, four-legged and two-legged that hunted the area had her blurting out, "Yes, yes I'll marry you." She waited in the room practically glued to the sofa until he came to retrieve her, praying the entire time she'd made the correct decision.

The last guest left at one in the morning. By two, Colette and Alexander were boarding his private jet, and three hours later they were married.

Colette kept her end of the bargain and allowed him to consummate the marriage. She curled into a ball afterwards, while hot silent tears slowly slid down her cheeks and she never uttered a sound, falling asleep within minutes.

Present Day - Colette

Colette trudged down the path from Mr. Stockwell's place as snow softly fell and turned the world around her into a fairyland. Her soul ached too much to appreciate the sparkling magic. Heartache is what she got from trying to be nice. If only she hadn't volunteered to help Mrs. Young, Alexander's widowed cook, deliver a pie three weeks back.

The auspicious occasion began when Mr. Stockwell's daughter blessed him that morning with a third grandchild. Alexander's cook had baked a pie in honor of the new grandbaby. The day was dark, cold, and windy, and as much as Cook wanted to take Mr. Stockwell the pie, she really hadn't wanted to go out in the weather. Colette had volunteered to go out; anything was better than being stuck in that big lonely house.

Mr. Stockwell loved the pie and was happy to show Colette the pictures his daughter had emailed him of the new baby. She made the appropriate noises of appreciation over the pictures of what looked like a large pink prune to her. Colette was about to leave when there was a commotion in Stockwell's kennels. He was well known for his prize Jack Russell's, winners not only in the ring but also in the field. Mr. Stockwell cursed under his breath and strode into the mélange of arguing dogs. He pulled out a small female, solid white except for some black and tan markings on her head, and tucked her under his arm until he cleared the run. Checking her over and finding no real damage, he placed her in an empty run alone. The little dog crawled to the farthest corner and sat shivering.

"What's wrong with her? Is she all right?" Colette's fingers gripped the wire of the run as she peered at the little dog.

"Nothing. Just the runt and that's enough for the pack."

"I'm sorry, I don't understand."

"She's the smallest, so they pick on her. If there's a problem in the pack, the pack takes it out on her."

"That isn't right."

"No, ma'am, it isn't, but then they're just animals that don't know people's rights and wrongs to things."

"Will they ever accept her?"

"Well, I'm starting to doubt it." Stockwell had taken off his hat and scratched his head in thought, then placed it back on his head.

"Maybe when she gets older?"

"Ma'am, she's a year and a half now, so her time's come and gone."

"What will happen to her?" Colette was sure

she'd already formed an idea as to the little dog's fate.

"If she can't fit into the pack, I'm gonna have to get rid of her."

Colette looked into Mr. Stockwell's face and knew what he meant. The little dog would be, in nicer terms, *put down* -- in plain language, killed. "Mr. Stockwell, please don't."

"Ma'am, I know you mean well, but I just can't have a dog that can't earn its keep."

"It's money then?"

"Well, yes, I don't mean to be hard about this..."

"No, of course not. I understand. Could you keep her just for a little bit while I try to find a home for her? I'll pay you."

"Now, ma'am, I don't want your money."

"I'm not offering charity; she needs to be boarded until a home can be found. She knows you and this place, so it makes sense to keep her here just until I find a home that will take her. And you'd be compensated for the boarding."

"Well now, I'm not sure. What would Mr. Neuville be saying about this?"

"He'd say you're a smart man. You're getting rid of a problem and making money at the same time. So we have a deal?"

"Well since you put it that way, I guess I can't say no."

"Good." Colette reached in her pocket and pulled out fifty dollars, still a great deal of money to her. Pocket change, Alexander would call it. She gave the money to Mr. Stockwell. Every day for the next three weeks, Colette visited the little dog, taking on the chores of feeding, cleaning up, and exercising her. She delighted in the care of the dog, her days finally having a purpose, and the little dog returned the attention tenfold.

Until this morning when she found the dog's empty pen.

She halted in her tracks and stomped her foot. Why, why had Mr. Stockwell sent Belle away and not let her say goodbye? It wasn't fair, she silently screamed in her head before her shoulders slumped.

Colette came in through the kitchen, making sure to wipe her feet. She wouldn't want to risk the wrath of Smithers, Alexander's major-domo.

A maid hurried to her, "Mrs. Neuville, there you are. Mr. Neuville is home early and inquiring about your whereabouts."

"Is he in his study?"

"No, ma'am, he's in the bedroom and instructed me to tell you to meet him there."

"Thank you, Noreen.

The woman gave her short bow and hurried away.

Colette glanced at the clock above the stove. It was only eleven. Alexander never came home during the day unless... He must have successfully closed a deal and came home to celebrate. She usually relished these intimate visits from her husband, but today all she wanted was to curl up in a ball and cry. As she climbed the stairs, she straightened her shoulders and thrust her chin up. It was just a dog, nothing important. There were thousands of dogs in the world. Mr. Stockwell had said Belle had gone to a good home, a loving home, so Colette should be happy for her. She wasn't. For the first time in her life, she was angry, angry at her life, her world, and the injustice that hung like a dank dark shroud over so much of her life wherever love or acceptance was concerned.

Colette sighed, glancing at the huge Christmas tree in one corner of the living room and paused on the stairs. Belle would have loved that tree, no doubt playing a game of hide-and-seek under the sweeping boughs, nudging the sparking ball-like decorations with her nose.

Sniffing away the pain, biting back the sob creeping up her throat, she dashed the tears from her checks with the back of her hand and reached for the bedroom doorknob.

Present – Alexander Neuville

Alexander glanced out the window. The snow was coming down harder, covering everything in a thick blanket. Where was she? He'd called her twice on her cell phone.

Glancing around the room, he studied his efforts. The vase of flowers looked great on the cupboard. Originally, he placed them on one of the nightstands. Then he thought better of it and moved the crystal container brimming with crisp white winter roses and blood-red poinsettias to higher ground on her dresser. Stepping over to the wall, he adjusted the dimmer switch on the chandelier, giving the room a softened appearance. He wanted everything to be perfect. For once, he could give Colette and himself the best Christmas ever. The last bit of hope swelled and grew in his heart for any type of family they'd have together.

Five Years Ago - Alexander

Alexander Neuville observed the waif doing her best to eat her weight and then some in hors d'oeuvres and his heart squeezed. Virginal was the word he thought of when he looked at her, despite the seductive siren red dress clinging to her few curves. Her enormous green eyes were made larger by fear in an overly pale face, even with the bit of makeup she wore. Who was she? After last month's gatecrasher, he'd thought that problem had been taken care of. Guess not. The new head of security started toward her, but he waved him away. He'd take care of this himself.

First he grasped the girl above the elbow, pulling her along while placing the plate in her hand on a table as they left the room. He didn't say another word until they reached his library.

He wasn't sure if the anger bubbling up from his gut was from finding out what she was or how she gotten in his house. Then she yanked the wind from his sails by blurting out her name. "Colette, Colette Carpenter."

He didn't hear the rest of what she said. The name hit him like a punch to the solar plexus. Carpenter, he knew that name from the papers. How could he not; it had been on the front page for weeks, every aspect of the family's life sprawled out in lewd detailed.

A loving couple who'd tried for eight years to have a baby and then had gone through another eight years of the adoption process finally granted children. They'd adopted the boy first, Keith, and then two years later, they'd adopted Colette. Over the next two decades Colette had been known as the quiet behaved one, and Keith the loud troubled one.

Most of her brother's troubles began with underage drinking and illegal drugs, later escalating to breaking and entering. Colette's parents did their best to help their adopted son, but the young man's problems came crashing down on the family one fateful day.

Keith could never hold down a job, while Colette, after her high school graduation, snapped up a part-time receptionist position. Her usual schedule was four hours a day, five days a week. But on *that* day, she'd worked three hours overtime. Three hours that had probably saved her life.

The local cops wanting a quick close to the case had tried to pin the deaths on the only living member of the family, her. But her employer, reluctant to become involved, finally came forward to confirm her alibi. Alexander had been disgusted by how quickly the financial sharks and the so-called relatives had picked the family's bones clean and disowned her. After that, Colette had quietly disappeared from public view, until tonight, when she'd shown up in his banquet room.

She dabbed at the tears running down her face, smudging her makeup with a napkin snapping his attention back to her.

Shame someone so young had fallen into the world's oldest profession. On the other hand, neither her family nor the town had reached out to her.

Some said he had the heart and soul of the devil -- of course never to his face; a few private friends knew better. Perhaps he could help her and himself.

A plan formulated in his mind. A crazy, wild plan. "Yes, marry me." Now that he'd said the words, he liked the idea immensely.

She stared at him, her jaw hanging open. But then she agreed, much to his surprise and satisfaction. He was so tired of being alone at the end of each day.

Alexander reached for the phone. He never bluffed, much to the chagrin of those he occasionally played poker with or had business dealings. In one respect, he'd won this hand with her; in another he'd lost big time.

Because, once they were married and he'd taken her to bed, he realized his mistake. He'd believed the sexy dress she wore, believed she was a prostitute, only to find out too quickly that she'd never known the touch of a man. Alexander lie in the bed in the dark long after, listening to his bride cry herself to sleep. The touch he'd shown her hadn't been gentle. Not that he'd been cruel, but he hadn't used the gentle hand a virgin needed. He never meant to hurt her but knew he had. A virgin was to be treated with coaxing, tenderness, patience, and persistence. None of which he'd shown in his haste to possess her, and he regretted his actions tenfold. From that moment on, Alexander made sure his actions and words were only kind to Colette.

Present Day – Alexander

Alexander checked his watch again, where was she? It didn't take that long to come from Stockwell's place. Should he start looking for her? He paced the bedroom floor a couple of times then crossed over to sit on the bed. The intricate carved foot post caught his attention much like it had caught his toe two weeks ago. Shaking his head, he grinned. Who'd have thought a piece of furniture and a little dog would play a part in saving his marriage.

Fourteen days ago, he'd stormed into their bedroom in a pisser of a mood. It had taken all of his control not to end the meeting with Weiss Corporation by taking their exec and beating his head into the conference table. Oh, he'd dealt with young, pompous asses like him before, and he'd dealt with this one. He made the little worm finalize the deal by paying Alexander's company twice as much for the building on the block plus all the closing costs. And the twerp hadn't even realized he'd been duped.

He usually craved the excitement of the game of high stakes acquisition, this contest of wills had been too easy, not a bit of fun; maybe he was losing his edge. Or maybe he was worrying just a little too much about how his wife was filling her days. Lately she'd been distant and quiet. His mind was filled with thoughts of her and what the problem could be. He didn't like the pictures running through his head. He was sure it wasn't another man; the household staff would have informed him. After all, they were loyal to him. Hell, with what he paid them, they had better be. Then just maybe they didn't know everything his wife did.

Angrily he tore off his jacket and tie, tossing them to one side. He sat down on the bed and yanked his shoes off, flinging them across the room and grunting with satisfaction when they thunked against the nearby wall. He stood and started for his dresser, but caught his sock-covered little toe on the bedpost foot. He didn't quite go down completely, grabbing the bedpost to stay the fall.

Alexander caught his breath from the sharp pain radiating from the injured toe and cursed, "Damn it all to hell!" Heavily he sat on the edge of the bed and checked to see if the digit was broken, joyous to find it not, only wrenched badly. He sat rubbing his foot. It was then he saw the loose trim on the footboard and sat for several minutes staring at it before realizing what was so odd about the board's placement.

Kneeling down, he tugged on the panel. It popped out easy enough, but when he tried to reattach it, it stuck on something. He bent further down, feeling with his hand as he attempted to wiggle the board into place and as he did so, he heard a soft thud. Reaching into the space, his fingers touched leather and he pulled the object out. A small journal about five inches by eight lay in his hand. He sat on the bedroom floor for several minutes just staring at the book. The bed and matching pieces were antiques. Had a previous owner hidden the book? Then after careful inspection, he knew the book's cover was too new. He debated for a moment or two whether to open the journal, then curiosity won out.

The handwriting inside was Colette's. He'd recognize the small neat penmanship anywhere, and he began to read. When he finished that one, he reached into the hidden compartment and found another, and another, and another.

Dear Journal, looked up from the book I was reading to find Alexander standing in the doorway watching me. His eyes blazed with passion -- so much indeed. I couldn't remember why I once thought them cold. He crossed the space between us, took the book from me, and laid it on the table beside the sofa. Next, he started kissing my mouth, then worked his way down my neck placing hot kisses and little nips as he went. He bit the buttons off my blouse and...

Alexander remembered that afternoon and how they'd made love before the fireplace in the library, drank champagne, and made love again and again.

He'd marveled at how willing and giving she'd been to him, delighting in his body as much as he in hers.

Dear Journal, well I'm starting to feel as if I'm able to contribute something to this marriage besides sex. Today Alexander came home and was pacing like a caged tiger in his office. He was snapping at the staff for no reason, which had them running for cover. He was so agitated it scared me, not for my safety because I know Alexander would never hurt me but for him. I was afraid he'd have a heart attack or something, so I knocked and went in to his office without him inviting me. At first he growled at me to get out, but I stood my ground and told him to_tell me, or someone, what was wrong before he burst a blood vessel, either that, or to just plain get over his mad. He stared at me for a moment, then started telling what was wrong. I listened as best I could. I tell you, Journal, I really didn't understand the ins and outs of what he rambled on about, it had to do with cost analysis, but I think that was ok, because what I believe he really wanted was just someone to vent too.

Alexander cringed at that memory. First, he'd been angry she'd entered his home office domain without an invitation. Then when she'd stood there in the middle of the room, hands on her hips, telling him to get his act together or else, he'd suddenly felt the need to tell her about his day. It had done him a world of good. He knew she didn't understand the technical aspects of the business problem he'd had that day, but she'd listened so attentively. She'd even at one point patted his hand and said something about it being all right. From that day on, he took a few minutes each evening to tell her about his day. And it dawned on him he'd never asked her about her days.

He read one journal after another, finding much more about his wife, her thoughts and feelings than he'd ever known. Alexander was stunned when he read she discovered she was in love. How she feared him finding out, afraid she would be tossed out into the street for daring to love him. This bit of news heartened him as well as saddened him.

Dear Journal, Well the doctor confirmed what I've suspected. I can't have children. Oh, he used a lot of fancy terms and medical mumbo jumbo, but what he said was I was barren. I thought I saw something. I'm not sure what, relief perhaps, in Alexander's face at the news. Maybe he's like the rest of the world and afraid I'd pass my bad blood on to his children if we had any.

She'd carefully hidden her thoughts, too. Ironic two people could live in a house for so many years, and yet, be nearly complete strangers to each other. He'd wanted to have children with her, and daydreamed about blond haired, green-eyed daughters that looked like their mother.

Finally, he came to the last in the five-year collection of journals and randomly opened it to an entry near the back of the book.

Dear Journal, went to Chez Jacques today for

lunch. They were offering the Périgord Mousse, that creamy and delectable mix of duck liver, forest, and cèpes mushrooms, and Armagnac brandy. They only offer it a few times a year, and ever since Alexander introduced me to it, I make sure to go when they have it on their menu and our anniversary. I was really looking forward to the_mousse and a light bowl of soup. The waiter had brought me the Périgord and the soup and left me to enjoy my lunch when I overheard Millicent Birdwell and her stuck-up friends talking about me. How stupid do they think I am? Never mind, Journal. I know how stupid they think I am -- I know why Alexander married me; he wanted something young, fresh, beautiful, and naive about the world. And he got a virgin to boot. Boldly went where... well you know what I mean, Journal. He didn't marry me because of my brain. I mean I know I'm not without some intelligence, and I know I'm not a log either. And once with his help, after I discovered sex could be nice, even fun, I've enjoyed all the things we've done together. But did Millicent have to use that term for all the world to hear? Trophy, oh she used the "F" word and I can't even write it in a journal. The word sounds like something you mount, I mean, kill and place on a wall. Stupid woman. I'd like to believe Alexander and I have been happy, but maybe I'm just deluding myself. Oh, well.

I went to see Belle today. Mr. Stockwell said he has a new litter that will need to be separated soon and that I must find her a new home quickly. I've looked and talked to so many people, but no one wants a dog that old or spayed. I wish I could ask

Alexander if I might have her, but I know what the answer would be. Besides stuffy old Smithers would have a heart attack if an animal left a hair or a footprint in his house. I wish that man would retire. I've never figured out why Alexander hired him to run this house.

Oh, Journal, sometimes when I'm holding Belle or playing with her, I dream what it would be like to have her here with me. I know she'd be quiet and wouldn't cause any trouble in the house. She could sleep at the foot of the bed or in one of those pretty beds just for dogs. It would be so nice to have someone to love me the way I love them and not have to hide my feelings.

Alexander skimmed the rest of the journal entries, then carefully placed them all back into the hidden compartment. A smile touched his mouth. So…his wife was in love with him. Hmmm, what should he do first? The smile ghosting his mouth broke out into a full-blown grin, then split as he started to laugh as he reached for the bedside phone.

Present Day
Colette And Alexander

"Grrrrrrr, bark, bark, bark, grrrrrrrr." The noise came from the other side of the door.

Colette's hand froze on the knob.

Next she heard Alexander's voice. "Shush, you silly ball of fur. She'll hear us and our surprise will be spoiled."

Colette turned the knob, slowly opened the door, and cautiously took a step inside.

"Ha, ha, ha." Alexander was on his back on the bed, trying, unsuccessfully, to hold off an eager tongue from an exuberantly happy Jack Russell. "Stop it, you silly critter. I'm loyal to one woman, and I only want her kisses, not yours." He started chuckling more as the dog concentrated on his neck. Suddenly the dog stopped, gave a yip of happiness, and tried to squirm out of Alexander's hands. Tucking the little dog against his chest, he sat up and laughed aloud at the look of astonishment on

Colette's face. "Hi, sweetheart."

"Ah, hi, what…"

The white and black bundle finally squirmed out of Alexander's hands and made a running jump from the bed into Colette's arms. With an umph of surprise, she caught the dog and took a closer look at it. "BELLE! Oh, Belle, it's really you. Oh, I was so worried about you. I thought…" It was then Colette's eyes met with Alexander's.

He rose to gather her and the dog in his arms and drew them over to sit back on the bed. "A little bird told me you two knew each other."

"Alexander… I don't know what to say…is Belle…"

"Yours, hopefully ours? I certainly hope so."

"Oh, Alexander." Colette leaned into him, and he covered her mouth with his. After a moment, Belle wriggled from between them to seat herself on the pillows.

"So you like the dog?"

"Oh, yes, but how did you… Did Mr. Stockwell tell you?"

"Not exactly. I'm afraid I need to ask your forgiveness about a thing or two." Alexander explained to a stunned Colette how he'd discovered her journals a few days before. Once she got over her embarrassment at his reading her personal thoughts and as he filled her in on some of his thoughts, she once again relaxed in his arms.

"I love you, Colette. I've loved you since I stood watching that scared young woman you once were trying to nonchalantly eat her way through a very large buffet. I grieved when we couldn't conceive children, and I've loved you for listening to me at the end of a lousy day. Most of all, I've loved coming into a room unnoticed and just watching you until you turned to look at me. The way your face lights up has always filled me with such joy." He took her hand and brought it to his mouth where he brushed his lips across her knuckles. "Can you ever forgive me for reading your journals?"

"Oh, Alexander, I love you, too." As she leaned into him for another kiss, something furry and warm wriggled in between them, demanding her share of the attention.

"I suppose you want in on this, huh, little dog?" Alexander stroked the dog's head.

"Woof." Belle stood on her hind legs trying to reach each of them with her tongue.

Alexander leaned over Belle to plant a kiss on Colette's nose. "So I guess this makes us a family?"

"I think we always were, it just took Belle to help us realize it. Oh, wait, what about Smithers?" Colette asked biting her lower lip.

"I sign the man's paycheck don't I?" snorted Alexander.

"Grrrrrrrr, bark, bark, bark, grrrrrrrr."

Alexander sighed, "I couldn't have said it better myself, Belle."

And they lived happily ever after.

The End

After reading

The Magic of the Christmas Flute

Catch a preview of

33 Days Til Christmas

From J. Paulette Forshey and Sizzler Editions

http://sizzlereditions.com/

She fell in love with an angel!

Archangel Gabriel is sent to Earth in human form to keep a woman, Zippy, safe for the next thirty-three days. He's not told why, only that he must protect her. After Zipporah is rescued by a handsome man when she's nearly run over, she quickly discovers he could use some saving of his own...especially when she realizes he's not a man after all.

As Gabriel starts feeling things he shouldn't, Zipporah, or Zippy as her friends call her, begins experiencing a rash of near-miss "accidents". His job more difficult than he imagined, Gabriel has to watch over Zippy without falling in love with her. But there's only so much an angel can do...

The Magic
of the
Christmas Flute

by J.Paulette Forshey

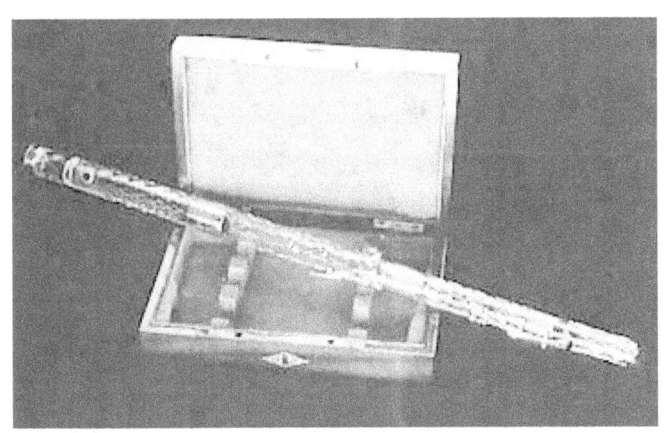

The Magic of the Christmas Flute

The wrench in Eli's hand slipped off the nut causing him to scrape his knuckles, the battered metal pulling him back to the present. "Damn it," he swore then hung his head, "Damn it all to Hell and back."

He brought the injured flesh to his mouth to sooth the damaged area. Raising his eyes toward Heaven he said, "Sorry, Momma, you raised me better."

Eli raised a hand to shield his eyes from the sun's glare and noted the long shadows spread across the ground. Callie was late. She should have been home earlier, knowing the blame was not all hers, he banged angrily on the tractor. If someone hadn't been filling his daughter's head with nonsense she'd be home by now. He wished he could take his hostility out on the real reason Callie was late. Movement at the front of the house caught his attention. His heart lifted, had Callie slipped in unnoticed? No, it wasn't his daughter who emerged from the structure. Eli clenched his jaw tight; it was the object of his anger, his father, slowly making his way out the front door and onto the porch. Granger sat heavily on the rickety porch swing and placed his canes to one side.

Eli snatched the worn handkerchief from his back pocket, wiping his brow. "Momma, how do I stop him from filling her head with ideas and dreams he knows will never be fulfilled? I don't have the money and it'll take her years to save up enough to buy the dang thing. Her dreams will be crushed in reality's bright light just like…you know Momma, you know."

Eli knew his father was trying to fill his daughter's head with the ideas and dreams he never was able to fulfill. He knew of the old flute in the pawnshop, and the costly price tag that went with it. Thankfully, he also knew it would take his young daughter Callie years to save up enough to buy such an instrument and by then her dreams would have dimmed in reality's bright light.

In the time since his mother's death Eli had made the farm look good. Crops were growing, his few chickens laid enough eggs for him with a few leftover to sell, the beef cow and pigs raised for slaughter had brought in a fare price and he'd even managed to put a new roof on the house. Only Eli and the bank knew what was in the black and what was in the red. The red was brighter than the black.

He took another swipe over his face with the cloth before jamming it in his back pocket; his mother's face swam before his eyes. She'd been gone nearly ten years but it still helped him to talk to her.

A flurry of pink and white raced down the lane then flew up the porch steps to disappear into the house. Eli paused his work on the ancient tractor to watch his daughter dash into their home and moments later race out again. She'd traded her dress for faded overalls, gave a quick kiss and hug to her grandfather before running to the barn and begin her chores. As she disappeared into the building's interior his heart sank a tiny bit, she hadn't noticed him. Her head was too much in the clouds these days. He slammed the wrench against the side of the tractor…on purpose this time.

*****

The conversation from months before with his precious angel, Callie, came rushing back. If only she hadn't seen the dang flute in the pawn shop window and if only her grandfather hadn't told her of the magical music the instrument could play.

"Papa, I could do jobs for the neighbors, sewing, sweeping, all kinds of things. I wouldn't keep all the money just a little of it. I'd give the rest to you so you wouldn't have to work so hard."

It broke his heart to hear his daughter speak of giving him money and he hated Granger even more for putting foolish ideas into Callie's head.

"Sweetheart, Daddy doesn't need your money and you're too young to be working on anything other than your schoolwork and your chores."

"But, Daddy, I'm a big girl, I can do both. I asked

Widow Jensen about helping her with mending she takes in and Mr. Flynn said he could use someone to sweep his storefront. Widow Jensen said she'd be happy for the help because her eyes aren't what they use to be and I could have a whole dime for everything I mended. And Mr. Flynn said he'd give me a quarter, a quarter Daddy, just for sweeping!" Callie's eyes were huge with hope and she rushed on to tell him, "Mr. Flynn said he'd pay a quarter because the store front was so big and got so dirty from all the people who came to the store. He said anyone who swept that much deserved a quarter."

"Callie," Eli pulled his daughter onto his lap holding her close. "Do you have any idea how many quarters and dimes you would need to buy that flute?"

"I know, Daddy, it would take lots of them." She'd gazed into his face with so much hopefulness quivering on hers with the want of that flute. "But I could do it, I really could, please Daddy, let me."

Eli remembered squeezing his eyes shut for a moment and then sighed. "Let me think about this, baby."

"I'm not a baby, Daddy," Callie said softly under her breath, her voice tinged with indignation but Eli had heard her nevertheless.

"No, you're not, but you'll always be my baby no matter how big you get or how old."

"Like you're grandpa's little boy?"

"Yes, I guess I am." He stared into her face and couldn't break her heart. "We'll try you working for Mr. Flynn and Widow Jensen, but if your grades or your chores suffer then that's, that. And I won't hear any arguments about it, do you hear me?"

"Yes, Daddy, yes!" Callie had given him a fierce hug, kissed his cheek then scooted off his lap. "I have to go tell grandpa!"

Eli had sighed and dropped his head knowing it was only a matter of time before his daughter's heart would be broken.

True to her word, Callie worked hard on her schoolwork, her chores, and her two jobs so that by the end of two weeks she earned two dollars and fifty cents plus the dimes from the widow. Eli suspected from the winks and smiles between Granger and Callie that her grandfather was helping her with her chores at home. However, Eli didn't let on. It was only right in his mind since his father had started this, that he help in some way.

The sun dipped lower in the sky making it difficult to see in the tractor's interior. Eli admitted defeat with the ancient machinery and picked up his tools then headed towards the tool shed. Granger wasn't on the front porch but Eli could hear his voice in the barn as he kept Callie company.

Later that night after supper was eaten, Callie tucked in bed and read her story Eli's one wish was to sit quietly with a cold glass of milk and a cookie. One look at his father's furrowed brow had him making a different choice.

"What's wrong Granger?" The past kept Eli from calling him father.

"Your daughter asked me if I'd ever met her momma."

"What did she say when you said no?"

"She just kind of sighed and when I asked her

why she wanted to know, she wanted to know if it was true her momma ran away and if it was her fault. I never asked son, never wanted to…well just thought it was none of my business."

Eli, a man of few words suddenly had words pouring out of him.

"About a couple of years after Mom died, I met Daisy. I bumped into her, literally, outside the general store. She was every bit as sunny and pretty as her namesake. I stammered an apology for not seeing her and nearly knocking her down. Daisy said if I really wanted to make it up to her I could pick her up at seven sharp Saturday and take her to the barn dance."

"You're a good looking young man, get your looks from your mother's side, I've wonder why there weren't more young women chasing after you."

"I've got Callie; I don't need any more females in my life."

"Speaking of Callie, what happened with her mother?"

"I didn't know anything about women, but Daisy was a good teacher and I was an eager student." Eli stared into the fire for several moments, his father not saying a word. "She was all silky, soft… softer than a new born chick, and she smelled like sunshine and meadow flowers. I couldn't get enough of her."

"Many a man has gone down that sweet path only to regret it later."

"We went to the dance and a picnic the next afternoon, from there it was long walks under the stars. I didn't even pause when she told me weeks later she was carrying Callie. I took her straight to the court house and married her."

"You did right by her then."

"Yes, I did, Momma taught me right and even before Daisy told me she was with child, I'd been working up the courage to ask her to marry me. I'd fallen for that angel."

Granger waited, not pushing the conversation and Eli knew it was time to get it all out.

"Birthing was hard on Daisy; she yelled and cursed me, the heavens, even God himself. When the baby came out and they tried to give her the little one, Daisy wanted nothing to do with her." Tears blurred his vision of the memory. "They handed that tiny bundle to me Dad, placed that squirming, cooing itsy-bitsy thing into these big old clumsy callused hands."

Eli held out his hands, smiling, still marveling at that day and continued, "She had Momma's mouth and turned up nose and I asked Daisy if we could call her Callie after momma's favorite flower the Calla Lilly. I thought since Daisy was named after a bloom she'd like that. She said she didn't care what her name was.

I should've seen right then things weren't right but all I could see was my beautiful daughter. She reached out her tiny hand and grabbed hold my finger so tight. I told her I'd never let her go and I'd protect her all her life."

"You've done a fine job with Callie, she's growing up into a fine young lady. Your momma would be proud of you."

"I had to do my best by her, seems her momma married me because she thought I had money in the bank not because she had feelings for me, or Callie." Eli sat still for a moment lost in the past. "Life was harder trying to feed three mouths but I didn't care, I had my angels right here on Earth. Then one day I came home for the noon meal, the house was empty of Daisy and her things, and Callie was crying in her crib, a note pinned to her blanket. My wife had left me."

"What did the note say?"

"I won't repeat it all, but never knew a gal so pretty could hold a bucket of venom in her."

"I'm sorry son; it's a shame that some of the prettiest things are the most nasty."

Eli nodded agreeing. "Daisy said she had enough of living in poverty, she was tired of my, well me pestering her, and I could have the kid. She said plain enough she didn't know if Callie was mine or not but she wanted nothing to do with either of us." Eli fixed his gaze on his father's. "Callie is mine, I know so in my heart and if anyone dares to question her parentage…"

"Our Callie girl is the spit'n image of her grandmother, no doubt in my mind she's an Ashwood."

"I appreciate the help you've given when I had to be in the fields or tending the animals."

"No need to thank me, that's what kin does."

"Then why did you leave Momma? Why didn't you take her with you? The missing of you ate at her like a cancer." The dam Eli built stone by stone to protect himself began to crumble. "Momma worked herself to death trying to keep this damnable farm going. While you drifted from one saloon to the next playing your music and following an empty dream of fame and fortune. Day and night, Momma worked until I was old enough to help take most of the burden from her when I wasn't in school. She'd insisted I have a decent education and she delighted in my meager scholastic accomplishments, though she never saw them that way. I remember her smile, tired by the day's work, the way her mouth turned up in a joy that spread to her eyes when I told her of what I learned that day or read to her. Once I worked up the courage to ask her why she didn't leave you to find a better husband — a better life.

She told me she didn't leave because she loved you and the gift you'd given her. I remember spreading my arms wide inside this house, more a shack, with rooms divided only by hung material and asked bewildered, 'What gift?' Momma leaned forward brushing a lock of hair away from my face, ran her fingers across my brow soothingly and told me that I was her gift of love and she'd never trade that for all the comfort or wealth in the world."

Granger trembled, Eli knew not from what and then his father answered.

"I *asked* her. God in heaven, I asked and I pleaded. I asked your mother, my sweet Juliet to come with me, but she wouldn't. Her dreams were here she said, you and this farm, and this was where she wanted to stay. I stayed away because of my sweet Julie, don't you understand boy? She had such high hopes for me and my music, I couldn't let her

41

down, I just couldn't. I didn't come home because I was a failure and yet I kept trying to make it and make her proud. I just couldn't come home empty handed."

"She wouldn't have cared, all she wanted was you to come home. I never understood it; don't understand it now, but you were riches enough for her. Was it because of me?"

"God no, boy, it was never because of you. I loved you too. I still love you. You're the only part of her I have left." Granger smiled. "You and our Callie, I swear she has your mother's smile."

"Yes, she does. Momma would have loved and spoiled her."

"Did your momma, my Juliet, did she go easy?"

"She went peaceful in her sleep. I woke that morning to a stifling stillness in the house, the kind that makes the hair on your neck stand up. Momma lay on her back, hands folded across her middle. Her face was whiter than the sheets around her and the heart on her cheek a pale pink. I knew she'd gone."

"I use to tease her that little mark was a kiss from the angels." Granger wiped the dampness from his eyes. "Miserable day when it came to bury her, with all that hard rain and cold wind, but the service, why you did good by her with it. The minister did a fine job, too."

Eli stared into the fire and an image of a battered old car driving up with two men in it swam before his eyes. He'd watched his father make his way up the hillside. Eli tried for once to see the man his mother had loved so fiercely but he couldn't. He saw only the breaker of promises, the dreamer, the absent husband and father. The image faded leaving the men to sit, lost in their own memories, and being men, they soon became embarrassed at their perceived weaknesses and said no more.

That was the last time they spoke together of Juliet but each spoke volumes when Callie wanted to know things about her grandmother. Though on the subject of Callie's mother, the two men spun tales of dragons, knights in shining armor and a princess being carried away to faraway lands.

*****

Callie sat counting her money again and again; a month had gone by then another, then six. Each time she counted it, it was the same, a pittance compared with the amount she needed. She sighed, this was going to be harder than she'd thought but then she remembered why she was doing this. Callie carefully placed her coins back inside the jar she kept them in and tucked it under her bed for safekeeping. She climbed into bed and pulled the covers up to her chin and as she drifted off to sleep, she repeated to herself, "I can do this, yes, I can do this!"

Callie was awakened by hushed urgent voices in the night, she slid out of bed and careful not to make it squeak, opened her bedroom door. Doc Westland was in the kitchen talking to her father.

"He'll need this medicine, Eli." Doc Westland handed a bottle of dark liquid to her father. "Have him take it twice a day."

"How long will this last, doc?"

"Should last a couple of weeks then you'll need more."

"Doc, it's not that... I mean... he needs this and I owe it to my mother to make sure he gets it... it's just."

"I'll get you more, Eli. I know how it is; you don't worry about paying me. I know when you're able, you will."

"Doc... I..."

"How's that little girl of yours? I hear she's doing well with her studies, takes after her grandmother and you with the books, huh?"

"Callie's, a good girl, she's my light." Eli smiled.

In the shadows across the room, Callie heard coughing, hard and sharp, it came from her grandfather's room.

Doc Westland put his hand on her father's shoulder, "Go now, he needs you." Doc shrugged on his overcoat and reached for the doorknob, resting his hand there. "Eli, he wasn't and isn't a bad man, he's just a man. He loved her and he loves you and your daughter with all his heart."

Callie saw her father swallow hard and shake his head in agreement then turned for her grandfather's room.

The doctor stepped out into the night.

Callie didn't even think twice. She turned and reached under her bed, grabbing the jar full of coins. She swung the bedroom door open ignoring the protesting squeal as she dashed to the front door and jerked it open. Doc Westland had just started to pull away but she saw him look in his rear mirror making eye contact with her.

"Callie, child what are you doing out here?" He had opened the car door and stepped out. "You'll catch your death out here."

"Grandpa needs medicine doesn't he?"

Doctor Westland looked down at the jar full of coins in her hands. "Yes, your grandfather is going to need medicine, but we need to get you back inside before you come down with something." He picked her up and started towards the front door.

"Doc Westland, no, I don't want Daddy or Grandpa to know."

He paused on the steps, "You don't want them to know you came out here?"

"No," she thrust the jar at him. "I don't want them to know about the money."

"Callie, honey, I can't take your money."

"But you have too, Daddy needs Grandpa and Grandpa needs Daddy."

Doctor Westland opened and closed his mouth. "Callie, aren't you saving this money for something else?"

"I was…" she took a deep breath and let it out slowly, "it was for something I thought I really wanted, but I want my grandpa more."

Doc Westland swallowed hard and turned his face from her for a moment but she noticed the glisten in his eyes. "Callie, I can't take your money."

"But you have too, for grandpa."

"Callie, what will you tell your dad and grandpa?"

"Can it be our secret? I'll get you more, I can still work at Mr. Flynn's and Widow Jensen's to help

J.Paulette Forshey

Daddy and Grandpa, they just don't need to know, do they? Daddy said doctors take an oath and he said when you take an oath you have to keep your word. And that's like keeping a secret isn't it?"

"Well, yes, I did take an oath and yes it's like keeping your word and secrets."

"Then you won't tell them will you?"

Doctor Westland shook his head. "No, I won't tell them."

"Good." She squirmed out of his arms onto the porch, handed him the jar and patted his hand. "Thank you for helping my grandpa."

"You're welcome."

"You should go home and go to sleep." Callie smiled up at the doctor.

"Yes, I should."

"Good night, Doc Westland." She stepped towards the door and gave him a little wave.

"Good night, Callie."

*****

Winter was cold and the snow was deep, but everyday Callie made her way from school to Mr. Flynn's store first, then spent an hour at Widow Jensen's, and finally dashing off for home. She no longer stopped at the pawnshop and even made sure not to walk on that side of the street. The town's people all noticed and through polite asking and the town's gossips knew about Granger's illness and his granddaughter's devotion to him and her father.

Many in the town made sure to just-happen-by Flynn's Mercantile or the Widow's house just as

Callie was leaving. A few used the excuse to inquire on Granger's health and visit with Eli to make sure Callie made it home on those cold snow filled winter nights. A few just happened to be on their way to town on the mornings Eli was tied to the farm when Callie was heading to school. It was funny too, how Mr. Flynn decided that the snow removal was worth an extra fifteen cents and that Widow Jensen suddenly had an onslaught of people's mending.

Every Friday when she got paid Callie dutifully marched over to Doc Westland's and handed her coins to him. Doc would hand her Granger's medicine and Callie, clutching the bottle to her chest, headed home.

*****

It didn't take long for Eli and Granger to notice Callie no longer talked about music except when they brought it up. They also noticed they no longer heard her counting her money or the sound of the coins being dropped into the jar. Of course, the increase of neighbors dropping by or them bringing Callie home hadn't gone past their notice either.

*****

"Your chest is sounding better Granger I do believe the medicine I prescribed is working."

"Doc, you and I both know my chest isn't getting any better, your medicine just makes it hurt a lot less." Granger reached over to a small bedside table and picked up a gold watch. "I want you to have this, Doc take it over to that pawn shop guy and get whatever you can for it. Use it towards your fee or the medicine."

"Granger I can't do that, besides Eli has been seeing to my bill and the medicine."

"Damn it, Doc, take the watch." Granger thrust the watch at him. "I've caused that boy enough trouble. I don't want him having to shoulder the responsibility of me now."

"Granger…"

"And don't think I don't know about Callie I've got eyes and ears. That girl works day and night and I know she's not saving her money for what she wants. She's wasting it on an old fool."

"She is using her money for what she wants."

"You'd think she'd hate me as much as Eli does. First I took Juliet's dreams, then his dreams and now I've taken hers." A coughing fit racked Granger's body. Doc Westland eased him back onto his pillow and helped him sip some water. Neither heard the door to Granger's room open.

*****

Eli had heard his father's words and knowing how his mother had loved the man even until her death it shamed him to think he could let his mother down by hating one of the two men she'd ever loved.

"Dad," Eli came into the room to stand by his father's bed. "I never hated you. Never understood you and maybe haven't liked you at times but I've never hated you." Eli reached down, took his father's hand in his, and knew in his heart that this was true. "She wouldn't have let me."

Granger shot the Doctor a hard look, "Tell him I was dying did you? That I didn't have much time left?"

"No, Dad he didn't say such a thing." Eli smiled and glanced over to the doctor. "I've just been figuring out what my daughter's been up to lately."

Doc Westland cleared his throat, "I don't know what either of you are talking about."

"And pigs fly." Eli shifted from one foot to the other, "Doc, I know I don't have any right asking this but it's coming on Christmas… I just can't let my baby girl not have something under that tree."

"I've been meaning to talk to you about that, it seems the pharmaceutical company has cut the price of the medicine they've been sending me lately. You've got a pretty good size credit right now on your account." Doc Westland raised his hand for Eli and Granger to be quiet when they both started to protest. "Why don't you come by tomorrow and I can give that money back to you, my way of saying Merry Christmas."

"Doc…."

"Now don't you two strong men get maudlin on me, you'll make me cry. Can't have something like that getting around now, can I?"

Granger squeezed Eli's hand and Eli returned the squeeze. "I'll be by tomorrow afternoon if that's ok with you."

"Tomorrow afternoon is fine." Doc nodded to Granger as he and Eli left the room.

"Thank you."

"You're welcome, Eli and you buy that little girl something nice."

"I will Doc and thank you again."

Doc Westland waved to Callie as he drove away. She was climbing out of Miss. Lorry's car at the time.

Callie ran up the steps and Eli caught her as she reached the porch and hauled her up into his arms. Callie squealed in delight.

"How's my girl today? Did she learn a lot at school?"

"I'm fine and we didn't learn anything today."

"You didn't?"

"Nope, Mizz Booth brought in a cake today and we ate it and sang songs and played games all day."

"You did? Was today special? I can't think why today would be special."

"Daddy you know what today was."

Eli had taken her into the house and was helping her take off her coat and boots.

"What's this I hear about today being special?" Granger made his way out of the bedroom and to the chair designated as his by the fire.

"Grandpa, we had cake, sang songs and played games all day."

"Well now, what kind of school are you sending our girl to Eli, that has them lully-gagging around all day?"

"Grandpa! You know what today was and so does Daddy. It's the last day of school for a whole two weeks! Christmas is coming!"

Both men had the good graces to look dismayed

then Eli gasped, "You mean Christmas is coming here now? I thought that wasn't for another couple of months yet?"

"I'm with you son, I thought it was a good six months from now."

"Oh, you two, you're tease'n me."

They made their dinner, laughed, and even sang a carol or two as a rift was mended between the two men for the sake of the child. The next few days were spent chopping down a tree, making and stringing popcorn on it and decorating the tiny home with colorful paper chains and boughs of pine. A few brightly wrapped gifts were tucked under the tree as well. Finally, it was Christmas Eve, and as they tucked Callie in for the night, both Eli and Granger silently wished there could be that one special gift under the tree for her.

*****

In the little town, a bell rang as the door to the pawn shop opened.

"Hello, welcome to Shepler's Shop of slightly used odds and ends. How may I help you, dear lady?"

"I'm here about the flute you have in the window."

"Why yes." Mr. Shepler went to the window and lovingly picked up the case holding the flute. He was glad he'd taken the time the night before to polish the flute so that it shone brightly in the fading afternoon light. "It's of fine craftsmanship with a clear tone and…."

"I'll take it, please wrap it up."

"Don't you want to know the price?"

"No, it's of no consequence. Please use holiday paper if you have it, sir."

"Yes, yes, of course." Mr. Shepler took the woman's money and placed it in the register then walked over to carefully box and wrap the flute and its case.

Mr. Shepler handed the package to the lady and hurried to open the door for her. She thanked him and stepped out into the snow that had begun to swirl in small gust of wind. The wind blustered just then and Mr. Shepler turned his head to avoid the blast of cold air and snow. When he glanced out the door pane, the woman was gone. He started to walk to his backroom thinking a cup of hot tea would do him good when Doctor Westland, Mr. Flynn, the Widow Jensen and Rev. Hawthorn came hurrying inside.

"Oh, my but it sure is a terrible night out there," gasped Widow Jensen, "I don't mean to sound unkind but let us hurry and do this, gentlemen. I have no wish to be out in this night longer than necessary."

"Now, Widow Jensen, we told you we could handle this on our own and you could stay in your nice warm home."

Widow Jensen gave an unlady-like snort, "And leave this task up to men, I think not!"

Mr. Shepler looked from one to another, smiling, "Can I be of some help to you?"

Doctor Westland stepped forward, "Yes, you can. We've come to buy the flute you have in the window."

"And we'd like to wrap it in this paper." Mr. Flynn held up a roll of bright paper with sugar plum fairies dancing around sparkling shiny stars.

"Oh, my, oh my, oh my. I'm so sorry but I just sold that particular instrument to the lady who just left here. The one in the blue cape. Surely you saw her as you came up to the store?"

The four looked at each other then at Mr. Shepler.

"We have been gathered over at my office waiting for Rev. Hawthorn, we saw no lady, we saw no one coming or going on the streets for some time, sir." Widow Jensen spoke all most in a whisper.

"But you couldn't have missed her, she was quite striking. She had on a dark blue cape over a white gown. Her hair was so blond it reminded me of ripened wheat and woven in it were bits of some flower that was delicate and pink. I remember the flower because I thought it was so odd that she'd been able to find something that fragile in this weather."

"You said pink flowers...were they tiny?" Rev. Hawthorn chewed his lower lip. "And did she have a tiny birthmark here." He pointed to a spot just below his own left ear lobe. "In the shape of a heart?"

"Why yes, yes she did, it was quite enchanting." Mr. Shepler grinned the most he'd ever grinned.

The Widow Jensen gasped at this news and asked for a glass of water as Doc. Westland helped her into a chair. "It can't be, it just can't be," she whispered as she reached for the Reverend's hand.

"Did she say who the flute was for; was it for herself, perhaps?" Rev. Hawthorn patted the widow's hand as he spoke to Mr. Shepler.

"Why no, she didn't, I'm sorry but the subject never came up. Why is this so important? Ah, perhaps you all were trying to buy the gift for the same person?"

"What is it… who was the woman?" Mr. Flynn fairly squirmed were he stood and wrung his hands.

"Yes, Rev. Hawthorn you seem to know this woman and I thought I knew everyone in this area." Doc. Westland was starting to become annoyed.

"You wouldn't have remembered her as we knew her." The Reverend nodded to the Widow Jensen. "Millie here helped on her dress and I preformed the service. They were a handsome couple that spring day they wed."

"Who are we speaking of Reverend, enough of these riddles," snapped Mr. Flynn.

"The Ashwood's, Granger and Juliet."

"Reverend, are you saying Eli's mother, Juliet? Because that's not possible I personally pronounced her dead and not only attended but helped Eli with the funeral."

"I'm not saying anything except Mr. Shepler here has described how Juliet Wagner looked on her wedding day when she and Granger Ashwood said their vows."

"But how…" sputtered Mr. Flynn.

"It's Christmas gentlemen, when miracles from the heart are possible." The Widow Jensen rose to her feet with the help of Mr. Flynn and the good doctor. "Now, I think it's time we went to our nice warm homes. Doctor, Reverend, after we drop off Mr. Flynn, why don't I make you some of my famous eggnog?" She started towards the door and paused, "Mr. Shepler if you would like to join us we'd love to have you."

*****

Mr. Flynn couldn't hurry home fast enough to tell his wife of the evening's events. The Widow Jensen couldn't remember singing and drinking so much eggnog, since…well…since her Harry had passed away. And the bachelors three felt as if they were young boys once again with their families.

*****

Eli and Granger, still in their nightclothes, watched a very enthused Callie unwrap her gifts. Of course, since she'd dragged them out of bed shortly after the crack of dawn, Callie had been polite enough to make sure her father and grandfather had opened their gift from her first. Each had a new scarf and mittens knitted by Callie and neither would ever point out the dropped stitch here or there or that the mittens just might be a trifle too small.

Callie got a doll, a real doll not a rag doll from her father, the type of doll that closed its eyes when you laid it down. Her grandfather had made her a bed for the doll, the type of bed that rocked. Between the two men they had made bedclothes and

Callie would never tell them the covers were lopsided and a bit too long for the bed.

"Well I better get dressed and get out to that cow, she'll need milked soon. She doesn't know it's Christmas." Eli made for his room to change.

"Just a minute, son I need to have a word with you." Granger motioned Eli over to him.

Eli went over and sat on the hearth beside his father's chair. "What is it dad, do you need your medicine?"

"No, I'm fine. I… well darn it, I feel like a fool… but something is nagging me to tell you this." Granger glanced at Callie playing on the floor with her new doll and crib.

"What Dad, what?"

"I dreamed of your mother last night."

Eli laid a hand on his father's, "I dreamed of her too, last night."

"Did you now, how strange. She looked like she did on our wedding day. So young and beautiful, funny but when I woke up I could have sworn I smelled the scent of the flowers she wore in her hair that day."

"She wore a blue cape that day… I buried her in it." Eli swallowed hard.

"She still had it?"

"Yes, she kept it for special occasions. I thought it only right she have it to keep her warm…" Eli turned his head for a minute not wanting his father or daughter to see the tears glistening in his eyes. "I just couldn't put her in the cold ground without something to keep her warm."

Granger patted Eli's hand and unlike him, let the

tears travel down his face. "She raised you right... I should have been here to help her."

"Dad, she was happy and she knew you were happy and... well she made a good life for us here. I was... I am... happy."

The wind chose to rattle the door just then and the cow in the barn mooed low and long.

"Guess, I better get out there before she comes looking for me." Eli laughed, as he stood then paused. "Did she say anything to you, Dad?"

Granger's head snapped up to look into Eli's face. "Yes, she did. She told me to be happy."

"Funny, that's what she said to me." Eli raised an eyebrow in surprise.

A few minutes later Granger was starting breakfast as Eli headed for the door.

"See if those chickens did their job, we're getting low on eggs."

"I'll stop by the smoke house and bring in that ham, it should taste good by now as long as I've had it curing." Eli opened the door, and then nearly stepped on the package lying there. "What's this?"

He bent down and picked up the brightly wrapped parcel. "Well looks like someone stopped by and left this, wonder why they didn't knock?"

"Who's it for Daddy, who's it for?" Callie stood on her tiptoes trying not to be too eager.

"Well now here is a tag... it says..." Eli just stood there staring at the bit of paper.

"What is it boy? You're pale as a ghost. What's on that tag?" Granger hobbled over to look for himself. "Mother of ... it can't be."

"It's her handwriting... it is Dad... but it can't

be."

"It is boy, it is. I'd recognize her writing anywhere."

Callie reached up to wriggle the package out of her father's hands. "To my darling granddaughter, the light of our lives, with this gift, make light any burden your Daddy, Grandfather or you carry. Love Grandma." Callie carefully removed the wrapping and gazed at the leather box underneath. Slowly she undid the latches and holding her breath, lifted them. Nestled in faded red velvet lay a bright shiny flute.

"Daddy?" Callie was afraid to touch it, afraid it would fade away and this would be a dream.

Granger reached into the case, removed the pieces and began to put them together. "Now watch how I do this young lady." He showed Callie each piece in order. "This is how you put this together and you must do this right every time."

"Yes, Grandpa." Callie watched in awe as Granger assembled the flute. "Now you hold it like this."

"I know how to do that Grandpa I watched the flute player in the Fourth of July band."

Callie held the instrument up to her mouth.

Eli noticed a bit of white sticking from the edge of the red velvet and gently tugged on the paper.

"Dad…"

The sound of panic in Eli's voice had Granger and Callie's attention immediately.

"What is it, what does it say?" Granger started towards his son.

"It reads, 'To my darling daughter Juliet, may

this lift all your burdens. Love Father."

Granger reached for the paper, "It's written on the stationery of Loren Wagner."

"But Dad, wasn't mom's father named Loren Wagner?"

"Yes." Granger sat down hard on the kitchen table's bench, "I never knew she played. She never said a word."

"I guess she wanted Callie to have it just as her father had wanted her to have it."

Eli bent down and lightly touched the metal his daughter held. "Callie I want you to do as your Grandfather tells you and you learn how to play this thing real well, ok?"

"Yes Daddy." Callie wasn't sure what was going on but something told her a miracle, not that she was sure what that was, but something very good had happened. "I'll learn and I'll play and I'll make all of us happy just like Grandma wanted."

*****

Later that evening, when the chores were taken care of and the last of the holiday was starting to fade, the faint, somewhat off key sounds of a music scale could be heard drifting from the small farmhouse. Three hearts swelled with love.

The End

33 Days Til Christmas

By J. Paulette Forshey

CHAPTER I

Gabriel Archer hunched his shoulders in his bomber jacket bringing the sheepskin collar up further on his bare neck. His gloveless hands were thrust deep in its pockets. The cold air nipped at the tip of his nose, while his boots crunched the snow and ice beneath them as he made his way among the shoppers. This was his third trip up and down the crowded sidewalks. The people were thick on both sides pushing, shoving, and bumping into each other without an "excuse me" or "sorry." Most grumbled under their breath, some didn't care and said one of several expletives common to the time. The masses seemed to have no thoughts on their minds other than finding that perfect gift, even if it meant maxing out their credit cards.

Yeah, they had the Christmas spirit all right.

He'd been sent here to find and protect one woman for the next thirty-three days. He hadn't seen any sign of her yet, and day was quickly turning to night. To make matters worse, The Boss sent him here without his powers. He was to do this job as a human. Who said The Boss didn't have a sense of humor? Many didn't think The Boss did, when actually, He had a good one, and at times it could be labeled as twisted. One word came to mind about The Boss's humor, platypus. Gabriel shook his head. He was still trying to figure that one out and why The Boss snorted and guffawed when the word platypus was uttered.

"Excuse me. Happy Holidays!"

The voice yanked him from his morose thoughts.

"Merry Christmas."

The voice, clear in the crisp air, rang out over the clash of bodies and traffic. Gabriel focused on the sweet sound and zeroed in on her voice. A dark blur caught his peripheral vision amidst the colorful shoppers snatching his attention away from her for a split second.

A terrified scream yanked him back. His assignment was flying through the air...straight into the path of an oncoming car.

Gabriel vaulted a bench, hit the ground running, and didn't think; he just dove. He was a warrior and fierce as they come.

His six foot six frame wrapped around her mere five foot seven one as he snatched her from the path of the car sliding on the ice straight for her. The throngs on the sidewalk had bumped her into its path.

Twisting his linebacker's bulk to take the impact of the landing, he smacked the frozen ground, breaking their fall. They skittered across the slippery road, causing other pedestrians to scatter out of the way. He slid with her atop him to finally land in a heap against a pile of snow left by a plow.

Great puffs of white escaped from his mouth as his inside warmth met the frigid outside air. He'd never seen his breath before. Holiday lights danced above his head from strings on lampposts blinking their celebratory colors. Quarter-sized snowflakes drifted lazily down on his dark chestnut hair like an afterthought to splat on his nose and cheeks.

All new experiences for him.

"Wow! That was some ride." She squirmed against him. "Hmm, sir, you can let go of me now." Gabriel lay on his back and dipped his chin to look at the bundle he held tight to his chest. Pansies. Big. Spring. Purple pansies, was his first thought. He'd never seen eyes that shade on a person. Her skin, almost translucent, made the dots of pink from the cold on her cheeks stand out like paint on a doll's face. A red and green knit cap adorned hair as black and shiny as a crow's wing, hair that swooped forward to brush and tickle his nose.

"Sir, are you okay?" said the bundle that wiggled against him, stirring things down below that shouldn't be stirring. After all, he was an angel, and angels weren't supposed to have stirrings. She was asking if he was okay, and he should be asking her that same question. For some reason the power of speech eluded him.

"Sir?" He sat up as she scooted off him.

"Did you hit your head?" Those eyes, huge with worry, searched his face.

Vanilla wafted to his nose and warm sugar cookies came to mind. Wait a minute, he'd never had a sugar cookie or any cookie for that matter, how did he...?

Her mittened hands framed his face, stealing the rest of his thought as she locked her gaze on his.

Gabriel raised his hand to cover hers.

"You have the most beautiful eyes," he gushed. Wait! When did he ever gush?

A smile with enough wattage to light up the Eastern Seaboard flashed before him, followed with a laugh reminiscent of silver bells.

"Come on let's get you on your feet. I don't think you have a concussion, and there doesn't appear to be any bleeding anywhere." She stood and placed her small hands under his left arm near the elbow, urging him up. Gabriel shook his head at the audacity of such a slender woman assisting him, and scrambled up. The bundle began dusting off the snow from his coat and pants, front and back.

Jaw clenched, eyes scrunched tightly shut, he tried willing the stirring away. It retreated, but to his mortification didn't completely dissipate. Thankfully, she didn't seem to notice.

"Well there, no worse for wear." She raised her face with those eyes to meet his and stuck out her hand. "Thank you for saving my life. I'm Zipporah, Zipporah Campbell, but everyone calls me Zippy."

"Moses's wife."

"Nope, not married." She stuck her tongue out to catch a snowflake, and Gabriel's groin tightened. He concentrated on what she was saying. "Do I really look that old?" Zipporah laughed as she smoothed a lock of hair from her face. "Don't answer that."

Gabriel stuffed his hands into his coat pockets suddenly unsure what to do with them. "I'm sorry, I didn't mean—it's an old name, one I haven't heard in a long time."

"No apology needed. I was being a smarty. Blame it on my mother, the wit and the name." She chuckled. "She had a weird sense of humor."

"Excuse me?"

"My family is, was, Wiccan, and Mom thought it was funny to name me after a person from the Bible."

"You're Wiccan?"

"Nope, got back at Mom for the name by switching sides," Zipporah giggled. "Don't worry, Mom liked irony, and she was happy I found something to believe in."

"So you do believe?"

"Of course, especially," Zipporah raised her hands and face to turn slowly letting the snowflakes hit her cheeks and tongue, "this time of year." Her eyes locked with his, and for a moment,

Gabriel thought he heard clear sweet music.

He realized they were standing in the middle of the sidewalk. She shivered; the temperature was dropping. He, on the other hand, felt rather warm.

He spotted an old-fashioned railroad car diner with the sign above reading 'Dave's' tucked between two buildings. It looked odd in the row of buildings because the rest towered over it. Gabriel grasped her arm, nearly pulling her off her feet in the wake of his lengthy stride. Zipporah's mittened hand beat against him.

"Hey, where do you think you're taking me?"

One good swat missed his arm and hit his nose. Gabriel stopped, nose tingling, but didn't let go of her. Those earlier gentle pools of purple now blazed and sparked. "Just because you save a person doesn't mean you can treat them like…"

One brow rose. "Like?"

"Well, I don't know, but nothing nice I'm sure." Zipporah stamped one foot and, slipped. He caught her. He put his arms around her in a flash pinning her to him causing that stirring again.

"I just wanted to get you inside." Two delicate brows rose.

"It's cold out; you're damp from the snow, I thought." Gabriel let go of her, stepped back to run a hand through his hair, then let the hand drop to his side. "You should be in where it's warm, have a bit to eat, and a hot drink to chase away the chill."

He thrust his hands back in his pockets. "Maybe I should take you to a hospital to be checked out."

Panic flashed in her face, but just as fast, determination replaced it.

"Nope, no hospitals, I'm fine." She tucked her arm in his. "By the way, I'll let you in on a little secret. A woman likes to be asked; the whole caveman thing of dragging a woman off and all is a real turn-off." With a tug, she started them toward the diner. "I know you saved my life and all, but I really hope you're the one buying. I'm broker than broke."

Gabriel adjusted his stride to match her smaller one. "Yes, of course."

That million-watt smile flashed at him again.

* * * *

Zipporah breathed deep, still trying to catch her breath from the scare and marathon dash to the eatery. The hunk, who'd moments ago saved her life, held the door open for her. Funny, he hadn't given her his name yet. She stepped into the warmth and wonderful aromas of the diner. Her mouth watered; despite everything, she still had a healthy appetite most days. He placed his hand to the small of her back, guiding her to an empty booth.

She caught her lower lip between her teeth, halting the tiny gasp before it escaped her mouth. His hand seared through all the layers of clothing and her winter coat. She felt the heat and strength of his touch as if she'd been standing there naked.

He leaned in, his breath tickling the delicate skin on her ear. "Are you all right?"

Zipporah didn't trust her voice at the moment and shook her head yes. A waitress found them a quiet booth; as they sat she handed them each a menu.

"Choose whatever you want." He tapped the plastic coated list with a finger.

"Thank you, Mr....?"

"Gabriel, Gabriel Archer."

"Gabriel, that's an angel's name, and just like a guardian angel, you saved my life." Zipporah placed her hand on his, which was resting on the table. A current like electricity zapped them both. Jerking their hands back, they laughed. While hers appeared to have bubbled up from nerves, his sounded forced, and she noted, didn't reach his eyes. Who was this man?

* * * *

Gabriel shifted in his seat. What the Hell was that? Where had it come from? Muscles in his arms, legs, and body tensed, ready for battle. He reached for his sword at his side and grabbed air. Jaw clenched, eyes narrowed, he searched the diner looking for whatever had caused the spark, while he remembered why he was sitting there defenseless. To protect the woman across from him, because it had been deemed she be allowed one more Christmas.

Gabriel snorted. The Boss thought he could

learn some, in His words, "valuable insight into His creations" by doing the job as one of them; his Boss might as well have tied both his hands and his feet.

* * * *

Zipporah's body sagged as the excitement and adrenaline started leaking from her. She rubbed her shoulder to ease the ache settling there. The sleepiness from the cancer pulled at her making her wish for a hot bath and her bed. She slumped in her seat. A large hand slipped under her chin gently lifting it. Caring eyes of chocolate brown with tiny gold flecks searched her face. Zipporah gave a weak smile.

"I'm okay, just a bit worn out. Thank you again for saving me."

"I haven't saved you."

Zipporah straighten in her seat. "Why did it sound like there was a „yet' after that sentence?"

Gabriel's shoulders lifted in a noncommittal shrug. "Let's get our order to go before you fall asleep here."

* * * *

One arm around her shoulders he guided her to a small, dark, late-model sedan. A wry grin touched his lips. The Boss had thought of everything even down to placing the memory of the car's location in his mind to the money in his pocket. Gabriel had frozen for a moment when the bill came before he took a breath and reached into his back pants pocket. Finding a wallet with cash, he said a little prayer of thanks. He thought he heard a chuckle in response, but it had come from the elderly, white- haired man in the booth behind them reading the paper.

Gabriel helped Zipporah into the car noting the dark circles under her eyes for the first time. He knew where she lived, but he couldn't tell her that. "Zipporah, what's your address?" She gave it to him while clutching the bag of food and leaned her head back on the headrest.

It wasn't that far, only a few streets down, and they arrived in a scant few minutes. She was fast asleep by the time they pulled in front of her apartment building. Gabriel opened the car door and scooped her up in his arms. She held a death grip on the take-out bag in her sleep. He walked up the two flights of stairs with her in his arms marveling at how light she was.

Gabriel reached the top of the steps with the sleeping woman in his arms, only to face the closed door of her apartment. He started to open the door with his mind then remembered he didn't have his powers. He was trying to figure out how to get her keys out of the messenger bag anchored across her body and not wake her, when his foot tapped the door. It swung open; so much for security.

One fleeting look of her dwelling assured him, and anyone who would bother to enter, she didn't have anything of value to steal. Seeing no conventional bed, he laid her down on what appeared to be two crib-sized mattresses shoved end to end in the corner. Besides being too small, they were too thin. They were better than the hard wooden floor, he guessed, but not by much.

He debated whether to leave her coat on for warmth, but decided against it, as there appeared to be enough blankets piled on the bed. The room's temperature was more or less acceptable. She never stirred when he removed her coat, hat, and boots or when he tucked the blankets around her. Gabriel sat on the floor against the opposite wall since there wasn't any furniture to speak of and took in the tiny room. It wasn't what one would call an efficiency apartment but more of a huge bathroom. Okay, large as the room couldn't be any more than eight by ten with a tiny six-by-eight bathroom attached. Crammed into that bathroom was a standard-sized, claw-foot tub and toilet. The sink was outside in the main room. Back in the larger room, her "bed" occupied a corner, and a miniature end table with the smallest microwave he'd ever seen was in the other with a hot plate and an eclectic cooler for a fridge. The last corner held an opaque plastic container with what appeared to be clothes neatly stored inside. Gabriel sat watching Zippy sleep.

With one sweeping glance he'd "toured" her entire living space.

*****

For the rest of the story: http://sizzlereditions.com/

or www.JPauletteForshey.com